saviour pirotta

Firebird

paintings by

catherine hyde

templar
books

In the shadow of King Vaslav's palace

was a marvellous garden, and in the middle of that garden stood a tree. On it grew golden-skinned apples, each one as dazzling as the sun. Walking in his garden one evening, King Vaslav noticed that some of his apples were missing.

"Guards! Someone is stealing my treasured fruit," declared the king.

Who could the culprit be?

"Sire," said the old gardener, "the thief is not a person but a magnificent bird with feathers of fire. Every night, it comes swooping down out of the sky and eats a golden apple."

"A firebird?" said the king's two elder sons, Dimitri and Vasili, with a laugh. "Do you still believe in fairy tales, old man, or are you trying to make fools of us all?"

"I want the thief caught, be it bird, animal or man," said the king. "Whoever brings the thief to me shall win a quarter of my kingdom."

A quarter of the kingdom? Prince Dimitri was determined to win such a valuable prize. That night he camped out under the apple tree, his sword across his lap. Come morning, however, he woke up to discover that the thief had struck while he'd been asleep.

The second night, Prince Vasili offered to guard the tree. But, used to an easy life in the palace, he too fell asleep, and the thief stole another of the golden-skinned apples.

The next evening the king's third son, Prince Ivan, said, "Papa, tonight it is my turn to try to catch the robber."

Now, everyone in the palace considered Ivan to be young and foolish.

"Why would you succeed where your brothers failed?" said the king. "Do not waste my time."

swooped down from the sky

But that night Prince Ivan hid behind a bush close to the apple tree. He took a flask of water with him, and every time he felt sleepy, he splashed cold water on his face.

Shortly after midnight, a rosy light shone over the garden, as if the sun were coming up. Then, just as the old gardener had said, a great bird with feathers that seemed to be made of fire swooped down from the sky, settled on the apple tree and started to peck at an apple.

Anyone else would simply have gaped in wonder. Not Ivan! Quick as a hare, he darted out from behind the bush and grabbed the firebird by her tail. The creature flapped and shrieked, beating her enormous wings to break free. She looked like a thousand sparklers, blazing together on Festival Night, but Ivan would not let go.

He held on until he heard a snap. The firebird had broken free and soared up into the sky, leaving only a single golden feather in Ivan's hand.

When Ivan showed the feather to his father, it lit up the entire throne room.

"So, the legend is true!" declared the king. "Whoever brings me the firebird will inherit half my kingdom."

Right away, Prince Dimitri set out to find the firebird. He rode on and on until he came to a crossroads at the edge of the kingdom. There he saw a huge rock on which was carved a warning:

Take the middle road and you will suffer hunger and cold.
Take the right road and you will live, though your horse will die.
Take the left road and you will die, though your horse will live.

"They all sound too dangerous," said Prince Dimitri, used to the sheltered life of a prince, and he galloped back to the palace.

The next day, Prince Vasili set out to catch the firebird. Not having any of his advisers to do his thinking for him, he was also scared by the warnings on the boulder and returned home to his father.

Then Prince Ivan said to the king, "Papa, may I go in search of the firebird too?"

"Why should you succeed where your older brothers have failed?" said King Vaslav. "Do not bother me, Ivan."

the feather

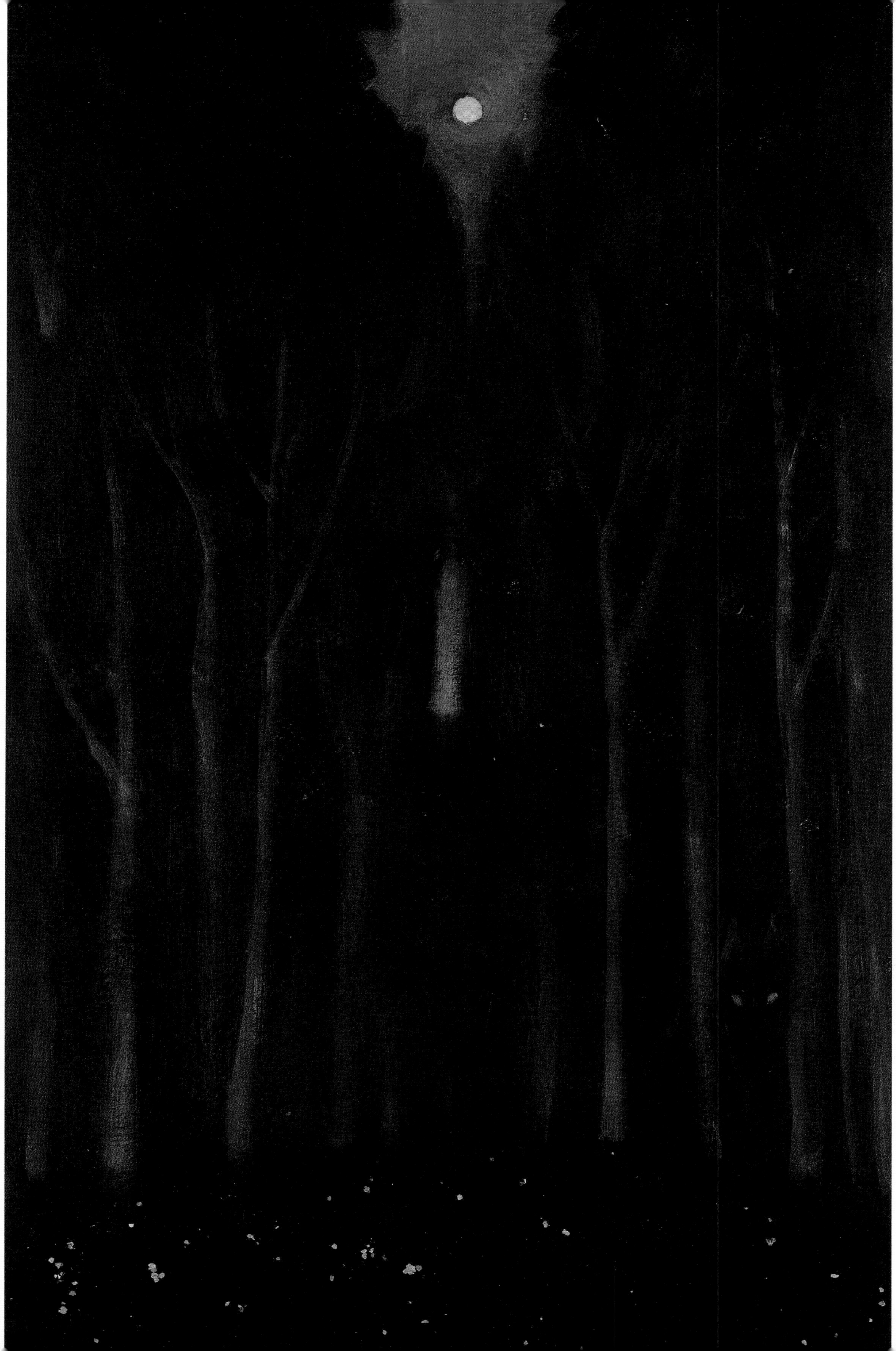

the edge of the kingdom

But Ivan saddled an old horse and rode out into the night. At the edge of the kingdom, he came to the boulder and read the warning.

I don't like being cold and hungry, thought Ivan, *so the middle road is not for me. And I don't want to die, so the road on the left is no good, either. There is no other way but to risk the road on the right.*

He'd hardly galloped past the boulder when he found himself in a dark and gloomy forest. He heard a growl, and a grey wolf, huge as a lion, leaped into his path. It knocked Ivan off his old horse, which it gobbled up in one mouthful.

"You are a brave lad," said Grey Wolf. "Anyone else would have turned back at the boulder. Climb onto my back, and I will take you wherever you want to go."

"Take me to the firebird," ordered Ivan, clambering onto Grey Wolf's back.

Away they sped, out of the gloomy forest and into a city. Grey Wolf stopped near a high wall, overgrown with ivy.

"On the other side of this wall is the garden of King Dolmat," said the wolf. "In the summer house you will find three birds in dazzling gold cages – the third cage holds the firebird. Take the firebird as she sleeps, but I warn you: leave the gold cage behind."

Ivan stole into the garden and found the three birds in the summer house, just as the wolf had described. He was about to put his hand inside the firebird's cage when he noticed that it was made of beaten gold. Surely it would be a pity to leave such a treasure behind? He tried lifting it off its hook, but immediately alarm bells rang all over the palace and he was captured by the king's guards.

"I see by your fine clothes that you are a prince," said King Dolmat. "Why would you try to steal my firebird?"

"It is your bird that is the thief," replied Ivan. "It took my father's golden apples and I was sent to bring it to justice."

"I should lock you up in prison," said King Dolmat, "but instead I shall send you on a mission. Beyond the mountains to the west lives King Afron. He promised me a horse with a golden mane, but never sent it. Bring me the horse and I'll give you the firebird and her cage."

its cage was made of beaten gold

So Ivan returned to the wolf and said, "Grey Wolf, take me to the horse with the golden mane."

Swifter than the wind, Grey Wolf carried Ivan out of the kingdom and beyond the mountains. There he came to a wall overgrown with roses.

"Behind this wall are King Afron's stables," said Grey Wolf. "Inside you'll find three horses asleep. One of them is the mare with the golden mane. Lead her out by her halter and she will not awake. But I warn you, Prince Ivan – do not touch her bridle."

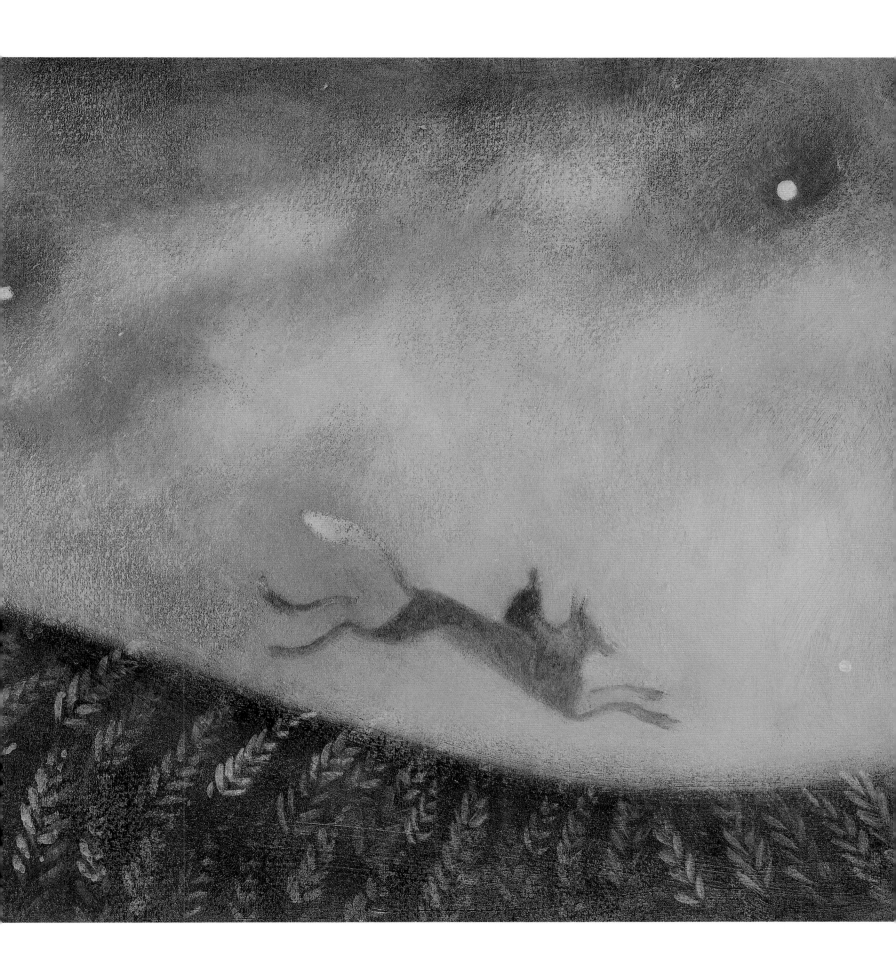

Ivan crept into the stables. He was leading the horse out by its halter when he noticed that the bridle was covered in diamonds. Surely he could not leave so great a prize behind? But as he lifted the bridle from its hook on the wall, alarms sounded, and once again Ivan was caught.

"I should send you to the gallows," said King Afron. "But I see by your soft hands that you are a man of noble blood, so instead I will ask you to do me a small favour. Beyond the river to the east lies the country of King Saltan. He promised to let me marry his beautiful daughter, Princess Helen, but now he refuses to send her. Bring me the princess and I will give you the horse and its bridle."

Once again, Prince Ivan returned to Grey Wolf and they galloped out of King Afron's country and across the mighty river until they reached King Saltan's realm. Grey Wolf stopped near a wall that was overgrown with pomegranates.

"Behind this wall sits Princess Helen, asleep with her book," said Grey Wolf. "Lead her out by the hand and she will not wake. But on no account are you to touch the book."

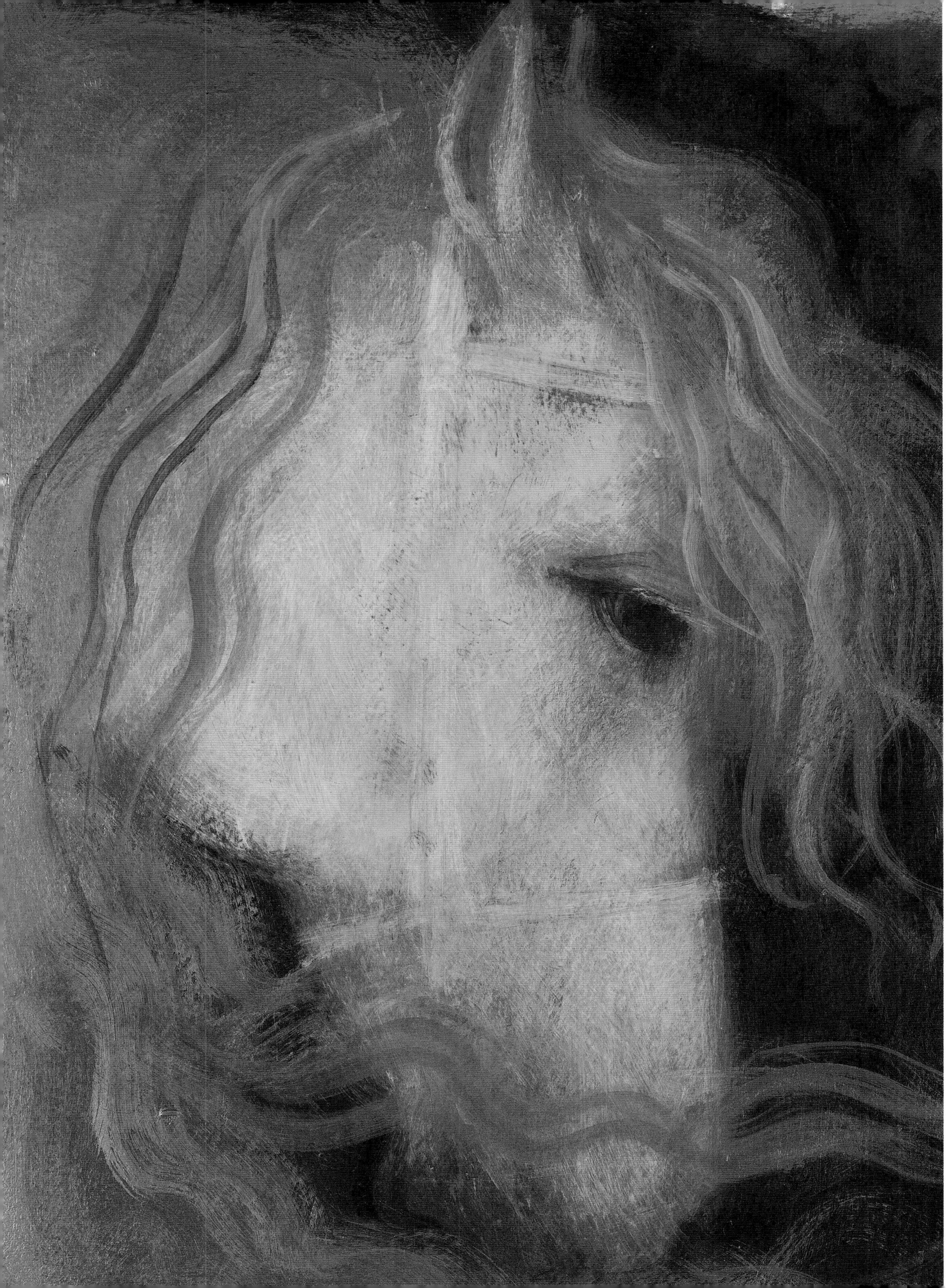

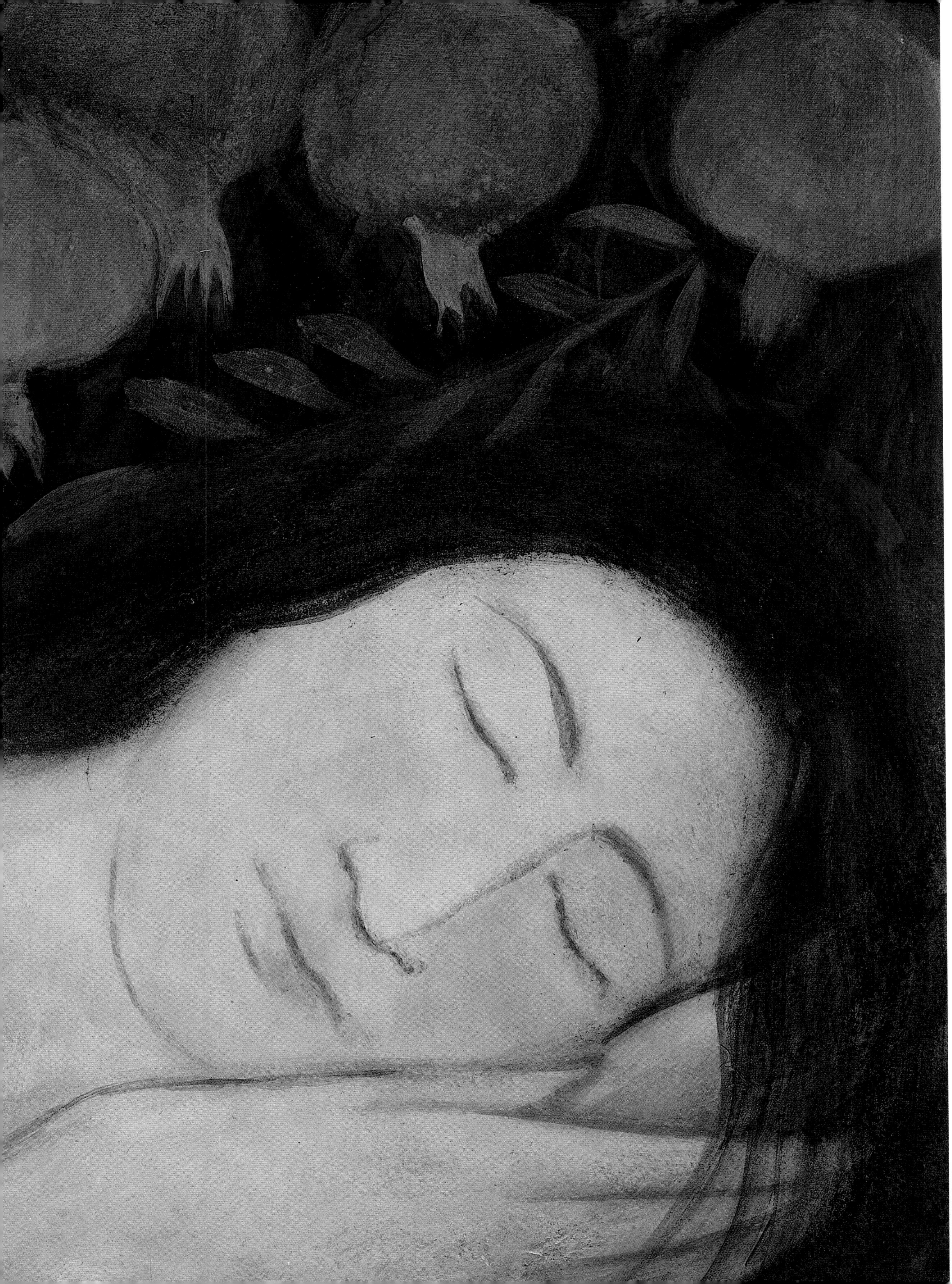

Prince Ivan was about to scale the wall when the wolf stopped him.

"Ivan, since you took no notice of my warnings about the birdcage or the bridle, I know you will not obey me this time, either. Go back along the road and wait for me there."

Prince Ivan waited, and at sundown Grey Wolf returned with the sleeping princess held gently in his mouth. He set her down on the grass and she opened her eyes.

"Don't be afraid," said Prince Ivan. "I've come to take you to your bridegroom."

she opened her eyes

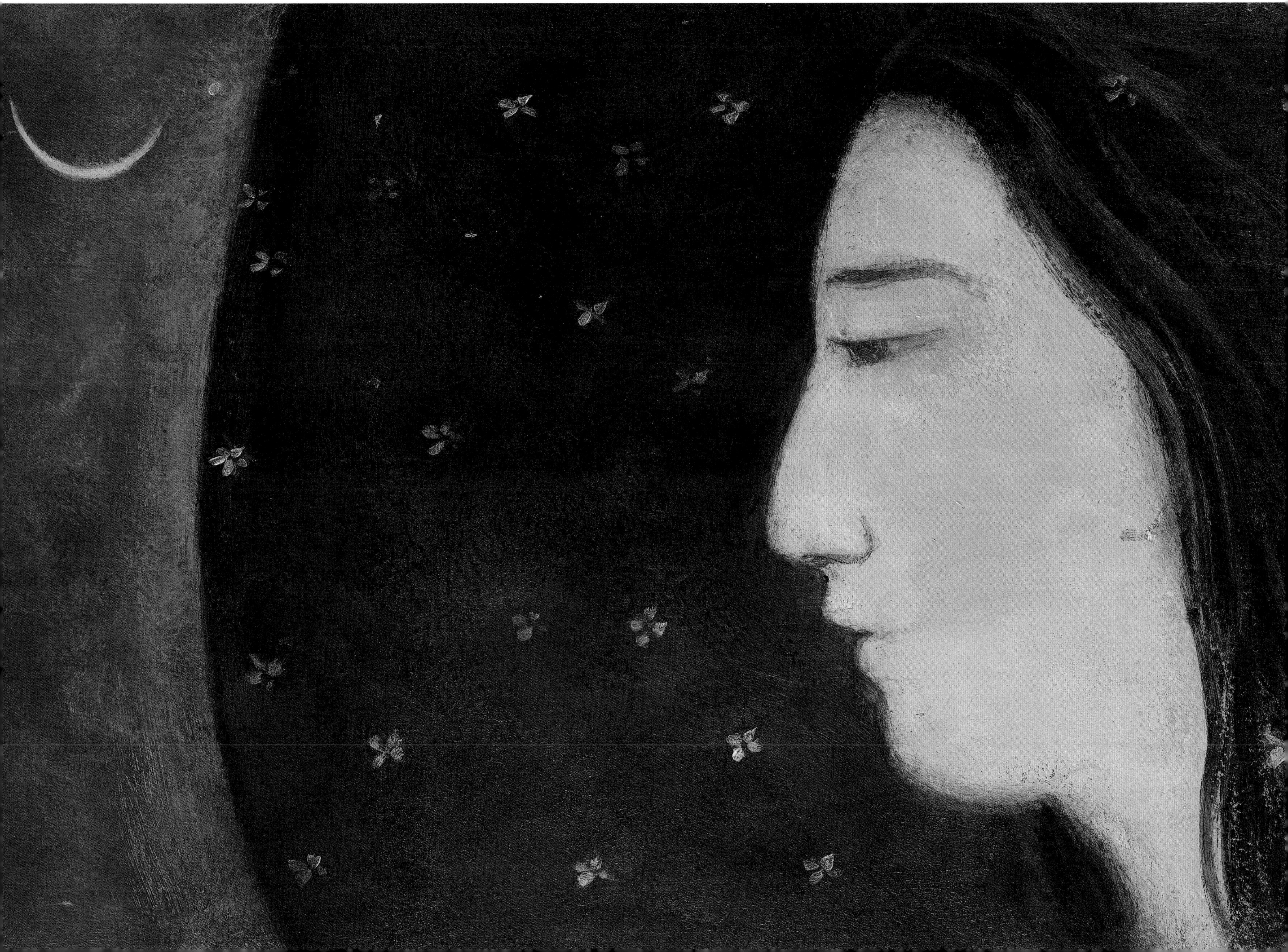

The two of them had barely climbed onto Grey Wolf's back, however, when they heard the blast of trumpets. Helen's maid had seen the wolf and raised the alarm. But no guard on horseback could outrun Grey Wolf and soon he was crossing the river into King Afron's country.

"Ivan, I don't love King Afron," whispered Princess Helen as they approached the palace.

"Whom do you love, then?" asked Prince Ivan.

"I love you, Ivan, and I believe you love me," replied Princess Helen.

Together the prince and princess turned to Grey Wolf. "Will you help us?" asked Ivan.

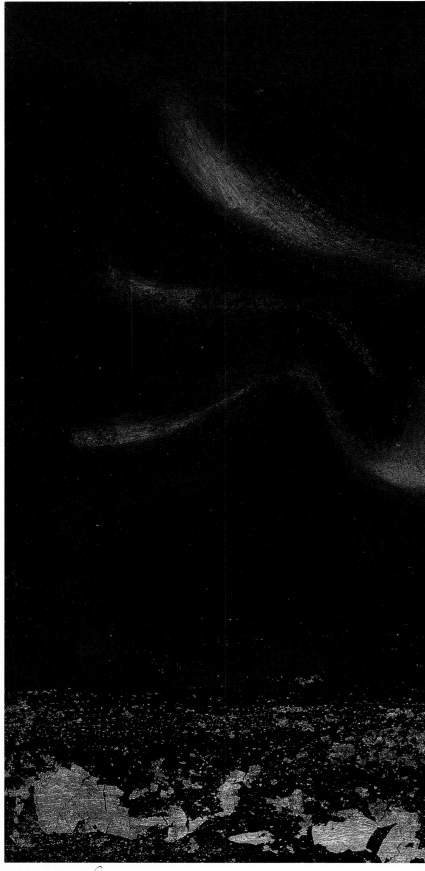

crossing the river

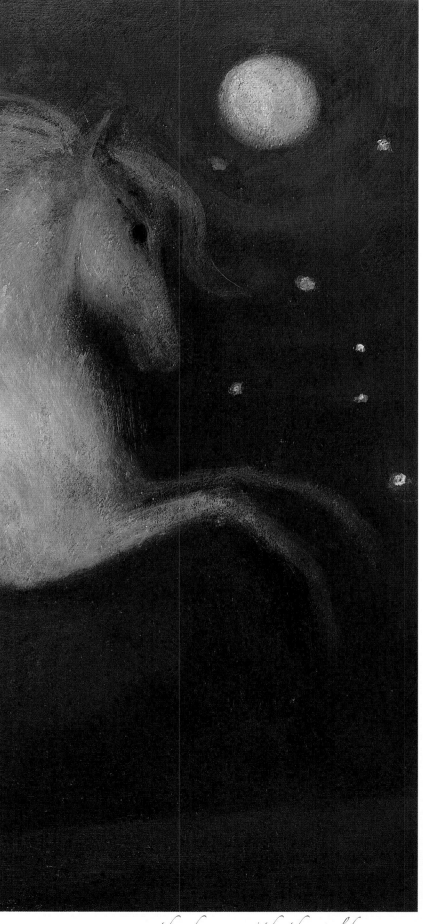

"I have already helped you more than enough, Prince Ivan," said Grey Wolf. "But we have grown to be friends, so I shall do what I can. Just promise me that the next time you see the full moon, you will call out my name."

Grey Wolf patted the damp earth with his paw and in an instant turned into a young woman who was identical to Princess Helen.

Ivan presented him to King Afron, who had no reason to suspect trickery. Claiming the horse with the golden mane, he then galloped back to the real Princess Helen, who had been hiding in a shepherd's hut outside the palace.

It had grown dark, and the prince and princess were well on their way to King Dolmat's castle when Ivan looked up at the moon and suddenly remembered the wolf.

"Grey Wolf! Grey Wolf!" he cried.

At his palace, King Afron was about to put a wedding ring on his bride's finger when – in a flash – she turned back into a snarling wolf and leaped over the palace wall. The king called for his guards, but no armed guard was a match for Grey Wolf. In no time at all, the wolf met up with Ivan and Helen near King Dolmat's palace.

Outside the palace, Ivan said to Grey Wolf, "Princess Helen does not want to part with the mare. Can you help us again?"

"Yes," replied Grey Wolf, "but Ivan, *please* do not forget this time to call my name when you see the full moon."

He changed himself into a horse exactly like the mare with the golden mane, and Ivan left him with King Dolmat in return for the firebird in its golden cage.

Later that night, while King Dolmat was riding near his castle, Ivan saw the full moon and called out, "Grey Wolf! Grey Wolf!" Instantly the king's horse changed into a wolf that leaped away into the forest.

he changed himself into a horse

King Dolmat summoned his guard, but what soldier can find a wolf in a dark forest? In no time at all, the three friends had met up once more.

When they came to the boulder at the crossroads, Grey Wolf said, "I fear the time has come for us to part."

Ivan and Helen both hugged Grey Wolf, who then slipped away into the shadows, never to be seen again.

That evening, King Vaslav welcomed them home with open arms. As a wedding present, he gave Ivan half of his kingdom, as well as the glorious firebird in her cage.

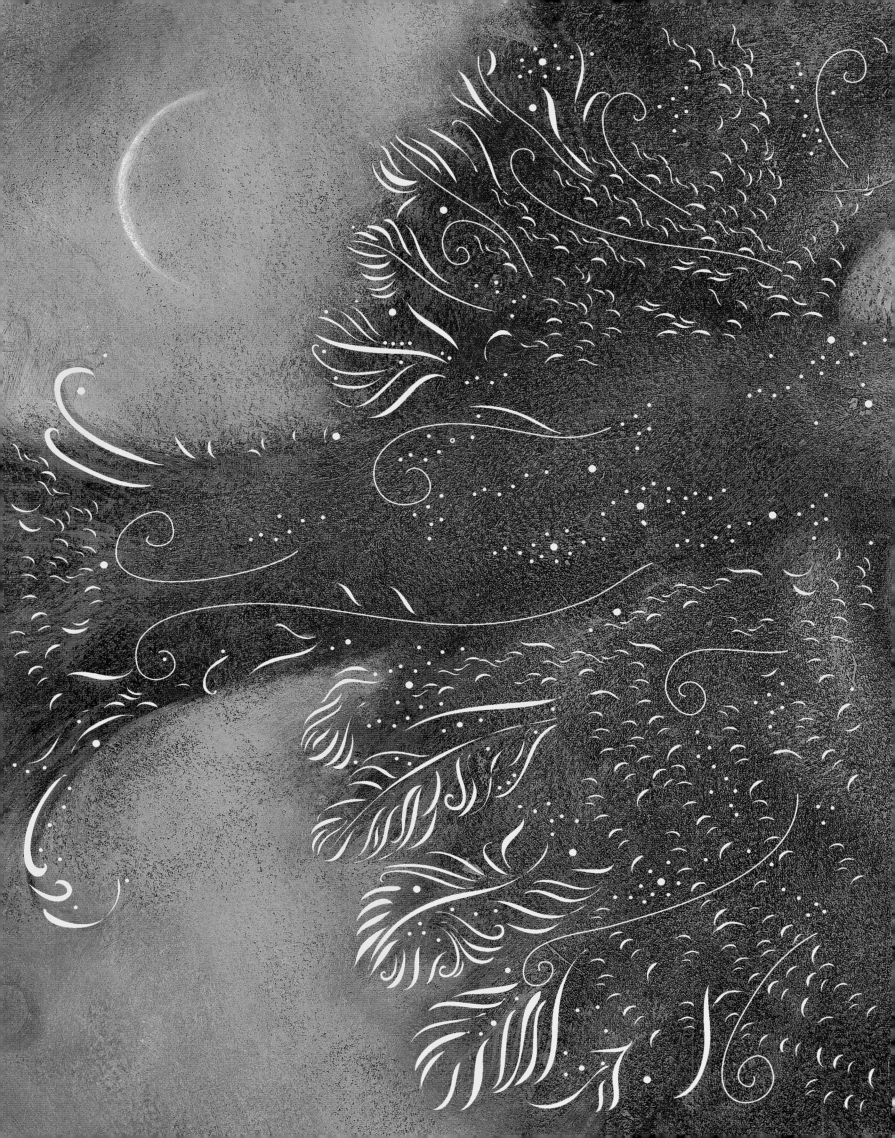

no one likes to live in a cage

But Prince Ivan decided to set the firebird free,

for no one likes

to live in a cage,

and she feasted on the golden-skinned apples

for the rest of her days.

The Story of the Firebird

The image of the bird of fire appears in the folk tales of many countries. The ancient Egyptians believed in a holy bird called the Bennu, said to be the soul of the sun-god Ra. It was sometimes depicted as a golden eagle with gold and red feathers. The Bennu was responsible for the Nile floods that brought prosperity to Egypt. The ancient Greeks, Phoenicians and Persians also had similar myths. The most popular stories about the firebird today come from Eastern Europe and Russia. Here the magical creature is often portrayed as a peacock with eyes in its golden feathers. In some versions, pearls fall from its beak every time it caws and its song brings a good harvest to the farmers.

The firebird in these tales is often the source of good fortune. But finding one of its glowing feathers forces the hero of the story to set off on a difficult quest, usually to capture the fabled creature at the behest of a king or father.

Many writers and artists have been inspired by stories about the firebird. Perhaps the most well known is Igor Stravinsky's music for the Russian ballet, The Firebird. First performed by the world-famous Ballet Russes in 1910, the story weaves together ideas from different versions of the tale of the firebird. Like the bird's feather, which can light up a whole room, this ballet is still holding audiences spellbound even a hundred years later!

the

❀ treasured fruit   ❀ he too fel

❀ the feather   ❀ the edge of the kingdom

❀ its cage was made of beaten gold

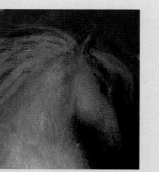

❀ leading the horse   ❀ Princess

❀ crossing the river   ❀ the

❀ the ring   ❀ he changed himself

❀ no one likes to live in a cage

paintings

sleep ❧ swooped down from the sky

out of the gloomy forest

swifter than the wind

Helen ❧ she opened her eyes

horse with the golden mane

into a horse ❧ a wedding

the golden-skinned apple

saviour pirotta is an award-winning author of nearly a hundred books for children including the wonderful retellings of CHILDREN'S STORIES FROM THE BIBLE for Templar Publishing. He has always been fascinated by fables and folk tales from all over the world and is a playwright as well as a children's book author. Born on the Mediterranean island of Malta, he now lives in Saltaire in West Yorkshire.

catherine hyde studied fine art in London and has since become a successful artist, with exhibitions nationwide. To create her paintings for each picture book, Catherine reads the story many times until she sees it "in terms of atmosphere and colour". Her first book, THE PRINCESS'S BLANKETS, was longlisted for the Kate Greenaway Medal in 2012. Catherine Hyde lives with her husband and daughters in Cornwall.

A TEMPLAR BOOK

First published in the UK in 2010 by Templar Books,
This softback edition published in 2014 by Templar Books,
an imprint of Bonnier Books UK,
The Plaza, 535 King's Road, London, SW10 0SZ
www.templarco.co.uk

www.bonnierbooks.co.uk

Illustration copyright © 2010 by Catherine Hyde • Text copyright © 2010 by Saviour Pirotta
Design copyright © 2010 by Templar Books.

3 5 7 9 10 8 6 4

ISBN 978-1-84877-151-2

Designed by Janie Louise Hunt • Edited by Libby Hamilton

Printed in Turkey